THE VIGIL

Also by Peter J. Dellolio

A Box of Crazy Toys

Bloodstream Is An Illusion Of Rubies Counting Fireplaces

Roller Coasters Made of Dream Space

THE VIGIL

PETER J. DELLOLIO

ISBN 979-8-9908030-6-0 (paperback)
ISBN 979-8-9908030-7-7 (ebook)

Published by Type Eighteen Books

For Luna

"A dog has the soul of a philosopher."

—Plato

Foreword

I wrote *The Vigil* as a kind of homage or paean to innocence. This book was one of those rare instances where everything mysteriously came together, like a precious gift from the gods. Not wanting to use a cliche, I must say that this work wrote itself. While many of my most cherished influences are evident, I hope to have honorably repaid debts to writers like Cocteau, Kafka, Beckett, Robbe-Grillet, Hawkes, and Joyce, *The Vigil* is first and foremost a requiem for a lost soul. I offer this work as a threnody from a father consumed by grief for the daughter he could not save. The work is a wailing ode for every parent who loses a child, framed within the tragic dimensions of Greek mythology and the sea.

SALTY BLANKETS OF crushed crabs. He wants to go elsewhere. Nothing glowing like the regal white lighthouse. Mystery and echo. Spiral staircase. A lighthouse staircase at night holds all the chanting mystery of the sea. Tonight the stinging air makes him wish it was all over. No more of this night, no more of this dream. Nothing to see in the gently unfolding waves except the slow-motion square dance of moon-soaked seaweed changing partners. Keeper of the beacon watching over Little Brewster Island. Unda like an imprisoned angel damned to a lifetime of the unstoppable wood from the weed-grown tree repeating his pitiful choruses of guilt and shame. Asking the indifferent stars to beg his drowned daughter to forgive him for lacking the stability of a non-weed-grown tree. Bits of flesh and scattered little claws of the crabs mangled after gulls' attack. But Unda cannot rescue himself from the sea. He cannot get outside of it. In his dreams he feels his daughter's wet fingers. In his palm the slippery cascade of coins she brings up from the ocean floor. All the ancient lighthouses from Alexandria. From Ostia. From Laodicea in Syria depicted on the coins falling into his hands like silt dripping from her hair. In his dreams he is keeper of The Tower Of Hercules. Nightly he battles Geryon and buries his head. He burns all fires and finds his flailing daughter calling for him in the black waves. When he awakes, he is back in the Boston Light, the coins slipping away from his grasp. They tumble one by one down the metal coiling steps, their descending chorus of resonance mocking Unda like a robotic chuckling. He awakes to the same desolation, the same nothingness of aching regret. The last coin spins out a double helix, its final wobbling like death throes flattened into silence.

"That was so long ago I can't even remember the poor girl's name."

"Who do you mean?"

"Unda's daughter, for God's sake!"

"You takin' the boat out tomorrow? Red sky out there tonight. Should be nice and clear. Good day for fishin'!"

"It was Georgia, remember now? Such a shame. And Unda still runs it, the lighthouse? I thought it was automated."

"Just couldn't think of her name. That's right. That's right. Georgia. No, Unda's still there but in a more or less superficial capacity, I guess you'd say. Coast Guard Auxiliary folks tend to it. They let him do some odds and ends. Probably feel a bit sorry for him."

"Yeah, I'll be goin' out for sure. Let me have a couple reels of that monofilament line while you're over by the poles."

"Going for the largemouth bass?"

"Yeah."

"So the poor soul is still up there? Damned shame about his daughter."

"Damn shame it is."

"Yeah."

...and you were wearing that pretty new dress we gave you for your birthday...nicest little dress I ever saw...like a peach and pink sunset...like a summer sunset behind Boston Light...like the sun squeezed the sky until all the juices came streaming out...steam rising out of my coffee cup...I had just poured myself another, and the bouncing wisps of hot vapor twisted around my fingers the way I imagined the rope coiling around my neck...did you know that...sweet Georgia?...I wanted you to know how much I've wanted to hang myself from the tower...I should be at the bottom of the sea with you...say goodnight before you sleep...settle your salty blankets with my steady hand...I did not save you...the lighthouse knows...it mocks me...in my dreams I fly across the island like a banished gull...I see the circular beam of the tower light and it stares back at me with accusation...cold orb of its eye piercing through the saline haze of summer twilight...my little girl...my Georgia...do you hear me?...forgive me...forgive me...

Slowly interlocking fingers of knotted seaweed hide the secrets of the sea from the prying moonlight. Unda stares ahead from the tower. His endless vigil. Against one of the walls he has erected in his mind lies the coat of arms of Corunna. Fluttering shadows of brave soldiers' feet charging to battle. Unda is not among them. He does not receive the rewards of courage. The shadows flit past the coat of arms displaying the skull and crossbones of the slayed Geryon. The Tower of Hercules standing at the top. The tower suddenly dissolves like a child's sandcastle overwhelmed by waves at high tide. His daughter runs away, hiding behind one of the walls, afraid to know why he didn't rescue the castle, why he didn't rescue her. The racing shadows of Greek soldiers, running towards battle and victory, are like a flurry of punches from a superior boxer, pummeling Unda's spirit over and over. Kegel helmets gleaming. Soldiers' eyes glaring. Unda's pride is an artificial prize. Geryon arises, and only the true Hercules can slay him. Unda torments himself over his failure to save his daughter. He is like a maniacal film director composing the very nightmare scenes that tear at him, rending his conscience into hopeless pieces, like the dismembered crabs nudged along the shore by the dark tips of twirling seaweed.

...and that's why your mother left...you see...kept telling me I couldn't let go...blamed me for clinging to the past...how you drowned... it drove her away...but I know why she left...my fault...I was supposed to protect you...dear Georgia...I watch over the sea...there's a sweet harmony in my steady gaze each night...a sweet union with the paternal tower beam watching...guiding...there were so many nights...I repeated the words from the Psalms on so many nights after the sea took you away...where are you now?...the words of the Psalms are of no avail...He caused the storm to be still...so that the waves of the sea were hushed...feverishly repeated words...up in the tower...staring at the stars...there were no rough seas that night...no heavy seas clasping their destructive hands in gleeful anticipation of destruction and death...no...no...not like bad nights...seven on the Beaufort scale...near gale wind speed...thirty-two to thirty-eight miles per hour...no...no...wave height thirteen feet...I sounded the bell dear ...Georgia...your mother left a year after you died...

"That's the hell of it, you know. The boat was seaworthy. And she knew those waters. Christ, she spent her whole childhood playing by the lighthouse."

"What about a backup? Want a couple reels of Spectra?"

"Extreme Braid you mean?"

"As I recall the whole night was dead calm, flat sea. Full moon, too."

"You'll know right off if you get a bite on this line. Bites go right to the rod and reel. Braid's got almost no stretch."

"Damn right spooky about that night. Coast Guard never found her. God knows how many times Unda went out in the rowboat. His own flesh and blood—how can you blame the poor man, although it must have driven his wife away."

"Left him not too long after it happened, didn't she?"

"Got to watch out for that, though. With no stretch on the line, that damn hook will tear right out of the fish's mouth. Need a leader with a braided line. Give you some leeway there."

"That's right. Some flexibility."

Beating splinters of rain across the wide lighthouse window panels. Unda's mind fastens itself to the pounding. His eyes fixed upon the glass. He is in the ocean. Transported by the watery assault of the storm dissolving his consciousness the way a Sea Lamprey attaches the hellish suction of its circular mouth to the flesh of another fish. The ring of teeth like a disc of horn-shaped flags. Ring of fire from the circus, where Georgia laughed so much. His eyes steady on the road while heavy rain struck the windshield as she slept during the drive home. The conical cotton candy holder stuck to her face. The Sea Lamprey is a vicious master of the sea. It has attached itself to Unda. He sees the boat. He tries to swim there. He must find Georgia. Slowly he sinks, his hands eaten away by the predator fish with its seven pulsating pairs of gills. He cannot swim without hands. His pleading mind throws him back into the lighthouse, where he sits at his desk before a steaming coffee cup. The hot swirling vapors mock the ice-cold hatred he feels. Hatred of his failure. Hatred of his soul. Hatred of the tormenting thoughts of his daughter's death. Her boat was found, but where did she go? What happened? He begs Breogan's statue to search for her. He sees himself holding the gigantic Celtic shield. Massive disc of primordial stone. That will undo the savage secrecy of the deep. That will unleash the powers of tigers leaping through hoops of fire. One by one, the occluded openings on the sides of The Tower of Hercules evaporate as the stone turns to dust and an endless series of striped, fanged warriors leap out. They will resurrect his daughter. Summon her from the layers of sea mud and dark slime. The tigers will bring her back. He thinks of her joy when the animals jumped through the hoops. He sees her clapping furiously in her peach and pink dress, the circus lights on her face. He knows his sanity is a prisoner of the tide and ebbs away a little more each day.

Cape Cod girls
Ain't got no combs,
Heave away, haul away!
They comb their hair
With a codfish bone,
And we're bound away for Australia!

So heave her up, me bully bully boys,
Heave away, haul away!
Heave her up,
Why don't you make some noise?
And we're bound away for Australia!

"There you go! Now there you go!"

"Wasn't that the one you're singing? Used to hear Unda sing it to his daughter!"

"Whenever he had her, even in the stroller!"

"Man, did he have a horrid voice! Couldn't sing in tune if his mortal life depended on it!"

"Yes, it's true! Surely that is a fact!"

"But what a sight it was, him in town with Georgia, and she'd look up at him while he sang that shanty!"

"Beautiful girl. Beaming up at Unda, so enchanted by the song, even as a tiny thing—as if she knew the words!"

"He'd bring her by the tackle shop or along on grocery errands."

"She loved the part about the codfish bone, didn't she?"

"Always brightened up even more."

"And she had one—I mean, didn't he give her a bone that she ran through her hair whenever he sang that part?"

"Yeah, she did all right and smiled at him so big and bright. Like a sunrise."

"What a terrible shame he lost her to the sea."

"Lost her to the sea."

"Yeah, what a shame it was."

...and that's when I started calling you Lumen...my sweet happy Georgia...such a bright face...always a smile for me when I sang about those Cape Cod Girls...I still have that little codfish bone...it's right here with me in the tower...right there...next to my binoculars and the wooden radio...remember on Saturday nights how you loved to hear the big band music ...but that was when you were just a few years old...they don't have those radio concerts like they used to...sometimes when the wind is blowing hard and slapping against the tower glass...I can hear those clarinets and saxophones...I can hear the trumpet notes leaping across the cold stone floor in here...the way you tapped and scampered around when you heard the music...and I can see the cod bone looming up at me across the bay...as big as a leviathan from the Psalms...raising its monstrous head up...coming for me...it's my punishment...sweet Lumen...I have forsaken you...I don't deserve the sure footing and safety of dry land...I belong with you in the dead murk where no breaths are taken...where everything that moves in the mind is echoed by the motionlessness of the eternal seabed...that must become my grave...my face buried in the black mud will rejoice for a few beams of light...when you look upon me...Lumen...with your innocent eyes...with the glowing stars inside your unblinking eyes...

CAPE COD TIMES
LITTLE BREWSTER ISLAND

Tragedy at Sea

LITTLE BREWSTER ISLAND—Coast Guard patrols have ended a three-day search for Georgia Unda, who failed to return to the island after taking her father's boat out last week. Her father, Ralph Unda, the lighthouse keeper for Boston Light, said she put out to sea just before dusk and he watched the boat through his binoculars. He added that after she'd traveled approximately two nautical miles, a heavy rain set in, and he could no longer see the vessel clearly.

A spokesperson for the Coast Guard reported the boat was located about five miles to the east of Chatham. The motor was turned off, which had allowed the boat to drift eastward. There was no sign of Georgia or foul play of any kind. Nothing on the deck, inside the cabin, or on the exterior of the vessel appeared to have been disturbed or damaged.

Mr. Unda was utterly devastated and unable to respond to questions. He did say that Georgia was studying photography at college and had wanted to take sunset photographs on the water. She intended to turn around and come right back. Unda added that the storm seemed to come out of nowhere and he could no longer keep the boat in his sights.

The Theseus, purchased only last year, is said to be in perfect, seaworthy condition. Local authorities will be performing a routine forensic examination on the boat. Hopefully, this will help solve the mystery of Ms. Unda's disappearance.

The proud father who balanced little Georgia on his lap at the circus has become a hollow-eyed creature who begs the sea to return his daughter. Sometimes his supplications are uttered in hoarse whispers. Sometimes he screams, standing on the rocks at the base of the lighthouse. On foggy nights, the clammy saline mist insincerely embraces his face like the jaded, dismissive hands of a weary whore preparing for her next visitor. He wants to walk across the path of moonlight shining on the ocean, extending to the horizon like a hallowed road laid out by heavenly builders and meant only for him. The walls of the lighthouse are covered with his daughter's pictures. She loved to photograph the sea. Mostly at sunset. At twilight under the pathway of moonlight that Unda worships like a beggar held hostage by the shame of starvation. Like a man strapped to the electric chair watching the executioner's fingers tighten around the switch. Why does he dream of taking Georgia to the circus? He cannot understand his own thoughts anymore. The ringmaster stares at the ocean moonlight photos for hours. Sometimes the shimmering gray light turns into the lion tamer's sharp jacket, glimmering under the glaring lights. Sometimes the gliding white leotards of the swinging acrobats turn into the gentle swaying of moonlight rocking to-and-fro on the ocean. Unda takes little handfuls of sand from his pockets and sprinkles them across the lighthouse floor. He remembers the sawdust from the circus when he looks at the sand. He hears the thunderous trumpeting of the parading elephants. Sometimes he thinks the sea is testing his vigilance and will one day return his daughter. Sometimes he sees her wave-devoured body walking aimlessly along the moon path as it suddenly loses its shine and turns ashen and chalky. The ringmaster's red jacket dissolves into blood that inscribes Georgia's name in the sand on the lighthouse floor. He stares at Unda reproachfully, cracking his long whip against the coiled staircase. His pupils leave their irises and become little solid black balls tossed about by the laughing juggler. Unda knows his mind is haunted by his daughter's disappearance. No rational explanation could be found. The boat's motor was not damaged. There was no evidence of a crime. Georgia's camera was found by the steering wheel. No trace of blood on the deck or any sign of struggle. One of the clowns shakes his head, turning from Unda and slowly walking down the echoing metal steps. The loud flapping of his large clown shoes blends into the noise of waves breaking against the rocks. The repetition is mocking, like schoolyard taunts.

> You stilled the roaring of the seas, the
> pounding of their waves, and the tumult of the
> nations.
>
> You rule the raging sea; when its waves
> mount up, you still them.

...I was supposed to find you...my precious Lumen...I buoyed the spot where they discovered the boat...I rowed out there every night for weeks after you disappeared...gossip started about me... I was becoming unhinged...I didn't care...let them talk...let them look...it was part of what drove your mother away...the scandal...the shame...let them think what they want...let them say what they want...I am here...my dear Lumen...my light...we are watching over you...the Boston Light and I...the beacon is fixed on the buoy at night...see how I embrace you with the beam of white shooting across the sea?...remember our summer walks around the rocks at dusk during the full moon?...and the moon was that lovely pinkish orange color like your birthday dress...we looked at the moon and you thought it was a giant peach in the darkening sky...you always asked me how a peach that big got up there...remember what I used to tell you?...it always made you smile...I told you that the moon loved your dress so much...it wanted to look like you...the beautiful glowing gauze of pink and orange...all over the face of the moon...because you were out walking with your father...wearing such a pretty peach dress...making the moon jealous...making the moon want to look just like you...

"You sure did! You sure did!"

"You mean it's true? I heard right?"

"Yes, you did! Oh my Lord! That poor girl! It can't be! Can't be!"

"I thought somebody got it wrong! Maybe mixed her up with somebody else!"

"No, no! It's the Unda girl! It's Georgia all right! She put out last evening, 'bout an hour before dusk! Takin' some of her pictures, you know!"

"Like always!"

"Poor Ralph! Oh my God!"

"Like she does all the time, with one of those fancy cameras she uses!"

"I seen them. I know what you mean. With those long lenses."

"Telephoto they're called."

"Yeah, just like always!"

"But it's seven a.m. for God's sake!"

"And she ain't come back!"

"That's right! That's what I heard!"

"You heard right!"

"Poor man! Poor Unda!"

"Coast Guard's been out half the night!"

"Where's the Theseus? Where's the boat?"

"They brought her in, Coast Guard fellas! Around dawn, I believe!"

"Yeah!"

"And no sign of Georgia? No sign of her?"

"No, nothing. Nothing at all. Only one of her cameras. Found it all right. Next to the steering wheel."

"Unda was sick with worry. What a shame. She put out before dusk. Never came back."

"They had to restrain Unda. Had to hold him down 'cause when he saw the empty boat he knew for sure she was lost at sea. He snapped."

"God help the poor man!"

"Started yelling her name. Calling her 'Lumen' like he's done since she was little."

"They had to keep him away, off the boat. Waiting for the authorities to come."

"Had to keep him off the boat."

"'Lumen! Lumen!' he yelled. Kept calling her."

"Yeah."

"You heard right."

"Turn the radio up a bit. It's that shanty again."

"It's a blessing to hear it right now."

"Turn it up."

Cape Cod boys
Ain't got no sleds,
Heave away, haul away!
They ride down hills
On a codfish head.
And we're bound away for Australia!

So heave her up, me bully bully boys,
Heave away, haul away!
Heave her up,
Why don't you make some noise!
And we're bound away for Australia!

On the worst of nights, in his most feverish, tortured thoughts, Unda is certain that the daughters of Ceto, the three Gorgons and the three Graeae, beset his unfortunate daughter with all manner of ills, all forms of disaster and mayhem from the sea. He sees the madly writhing shadows of the terrifying sea-monsters spawned by Ceto. Their contortions sprawl across the white walls of the lighthouse. Transfixed and tormented, Unda watches them, sitting in his chair. He sees these demonic creatures of the sea using their silhouettes to deceive. As he stands, looking more closely, he thinks it is his own body that transforms into the dark outline of a hellish serpent, a fiendish whale, sent by Ceto to remind him he failed to protect his daughter. It is like awakening night after night to find himself behind the wheel of a runaway car, with mangled bodies, left broken and bloody in his wake. Each time his vehicle strikes someone, the loud, thick thud of metal slamming into bones and flesh becomes the pounding of his fist, pitifully and desperately slamming the deck of Georgia's boat, before the Coast Guard officers pulled him away as decently and humanely as possible. The row of white and red stripes on the badge of the ensign who escorted him off the boat became the candy-striped popcorn box from the circus. That was Unda's repeating thought that morning when the boat was found and returned without his sweet Lumen. Looking in a frenzy through the windshield of the mad vehicle careening past loft buildings with rows of large, semicircular windows, Unda sees his daughter standing behind each pane of glass, as though she were multiplied into all the residents of a Roman insula, standing and staring at the hapless Unda from their solemn stone apertures. When the Ensign leaned over to try and comfort Unda that morning, the striped insignia of his badge tilted downward the way the popcorn box had slipped out of Georgia's buttery fingers. She had looked over at her father with such a shocked and embarrassed expression as dozens of glistening puffs scattered across her lap and onto the sawdust floor. He made her feel worse. It was unfair to admonish her like that and he immediately regretted it. He wanted to buy her another popcorn but did not do so. In the grotesque images of seeing himself unable to control the speeding car, he watches his precious Lumen standing in all the windows, reproduced like graph quadrants from a fly's vision, sheepishly holding up an identical striped popcorn box, as though to make amends for dropping it at the circus.

> The sea is His, for he made it, and
> his hands formed the dry land.

> Here is the sea, great and wide, which
> teems with creatures innumerable, living things
> both small and great.

Grand darkness wet beyond all of time I am time what is taken what is given I am the sea without reason without passion pure energy of the night and ages all secrets begin and end with me I am every mystery everything begins and must end in me every contour of mind thoughts feelings hopes dreams articulated in my waves repeating shapes eternal rhythms unfolding manifestations of pitiful humanity in your search for the answers I am the ambition you reach for new lands you dream upon me I am the origin of life all the menace all the beauty all the endless cavernous unknown worlds deep within me a landscape of dissolving death all the rotting boards and iron of sunken ships collapsed into morose nothingness sequestered from the adventures of earth like the lighthouse keeper's daughter sweet Lumen I am the cruel court in which severe judgements and condemnations are handed out the vastness of my ocean kingdoms every age attempting to unwrap my secrets to try and claim the unknown they are all here none brought my inner life back to the surface they are here with Georgia I have claimed the Spanish Armada along with Kublai Khan's fleet all twisting ghosts next to Royal Mail Ship Empress of Ireland and the MS Estonia along with thousands of others since Eudoxus of Cyzicus yes even he is here a silent skull nodding slowly next to beautiful Georgia's hair waving in the decomposition of death like a sea anemone hiding its vicious poison.

...that day you found a dead sea gull on the rocks... the first time you saw a dead thing...you were so sad...how you cried...I was in the beacon...cleaning the mirrors...you kneeled with the bird in your hands...you wept as you carried it carefully all the way up the stairs to show me...you thought it was because of your dream the previous night...heavy fog coated the sky when I put you to bed...you wondered if the gulls would be safe... then you awoke crying...you were frightened...in your dream a gull crashed into the lighthouse... you wanted me to check...I assured you it was just a dream...I took you by the hand and led you back to bed...but the next day you held the limp creature in your hands...you cradled it against your chest...with your new pageboy haircut ...you looked like the little girl in *Child With a Dove*...remember dear Lumen?...we had gone to the Boston Museum of Arts...you fell in love with the painting so I bought a print ...we hung it on the wall to watch over the seagulls you said...your affinity with that girl in the painting...the gull's breast was damp with your tears...you would not relinquish it...no matter how tenderly I tried to cajole you...no...no...my sweet girl...my precious Lumen...the gull did not die because of your dream...do you pity me...my lost child...do you take pity on me...when your spirit...dripping with the deep darkness of the unforgiving sea...floats across this empty lighthouse and sees me touching the old poster...looking at that delicate child holding her dove with a coquettish expression...remembering the daughter paralyzed with guilt over the unfortunate seagull killed by the rough laws of nature...do you see an embodiment of your loving selfless soul in my own pain.......I was the lighthouse keeper...I was the lighthouse keeper...I could not save you...we buried the gull together and you took the painting off the wall and put it in your desk drawer...you never looked at it again...

"That's why nobody talks of it much, out of respect for that poor man."

"Nothing but pain and tragedy there."

"Pain and tragedy."

"How else could it have been? You know what I mean."

"That's true, I suppose. Can't get around it no how."

"No how."

"The girl wasn't pulled down to the sea bottom by Kraken."

"Or Cetus for that matter!"

"All right, I said we should keep some civility in our mouths. It ain't been more than a month since Unda had this sorrow put upon him."

"That long since they found the Theseus?"

"Just about. The *Cape Cod Times* article was four or five weeks ago."

"What you gettin' at? About that sorry girl? What's your point?"

"Kraken didn't get her! In bad taste, that's for sure."

"Alls I'm saying is her boat got towed in without a scratch on her. She was shipshape for sure, not a sign of flotsam and jetsam. From stem to stern not a trace of trouble."

"And like Unda said, she was in the offing. He could see the boat in the lighthouse beam after sunset."

"That's right. Georgia was takin' some sunset pictures."

"I know what you're gettin' at! I know! Guess it's been on everybody's mind."

"That's what I'm saying! Let's face facts here! The railing on the Theseus was almost four feet high. Georgia was a petite young lady."

"True enough."

"Stood maybe four-foot-ten?"

"I would say so. For sure!"

"And you don't slip off no boat deck with measurements like that!"

"Wasn't like she was out there in a rowboat and lost her balance."

"This ain't the sort of thing we ought to be talking about in the open like this. Ain't respectful."

"Ah c'mon, let's just say it!"

"So you think that poor troubled girl went out there to kill herself, don't you?"

"Didn't you say somebody overheard the sheriff talking to one of them Coast Guard fellas and they said something about findin' Georgia's clothes all folded and piled up nice and neat at the back of the boat?"

"I heard that too!"

"Seems like a strange way to take pictures, don't it?"

"True enough."

Oh dearest father how can I take away your pain?

Each night I send the wind across the bay.

The heavy sad wind filled with my tears for you.

I hear your slow steps on the lighthouse stairs.

I feel the mocking sorrow on every object you touch.

You always called me your light.

Your Lumen.

I would multiply the lighthouse beam.

To bring back that night for you.

See?

Look there in the offing!

My dear father.

A hundred beams of light illuminate the sea.

Like a thousand moments of supernatural sunrise.

A million suns burning across the black waves.

You see me and calmly nod.

I'm holding the rescued seagull.

Its beak nestled against my breast.

Salty feathers speckled with sand.

Can you see?

Now you must rest.

My suffering father.

Lear's broken heart is a trifle compared to your endless pain.

The night. Everything in the night haunts Unda. All the questions of that night. The endless questions like a thousand cuts. They come to pierce his flesh. If only he could bleed out and perish. But there is always more. Always more. The knives in his soul constantly asking what he cannot answer.

Why did she put out to sea so near dusk? What was she thinking? How could he let her go? Were there signs her obsessions had come back? Was she dreaming of the seagull again? What happened in the boat? Did she slip? Did she try to photograph something in the water and fall overboard? Is the Coast Guard keeping something confidential from him? Do the authorities have any new theories? Why didn't he stop her? Why couldn't he have seen that dropping her popcorn at the circus meant she would lose control of the wheel on the boat? Was she thinking of the dead seagull? Did she think it had smashed against the side of the boat in the darkness? Was it flailing in the mist-thick water off the stern? Why didn't he check the lazarette to make sure she had life jackets? Were they there? Why can he no longer bear to hear the crashing of the waves? Does he see her long beautiful hair flowing through each strand of curling sea foam? Is she there? Is she there? Why does he row out each night to the spot in the offing where the deserted boat was found? Why does he unfurl the poster of *Child with a Dove* each night? Why does he hear her voice in the little pockets of wind through the lighthouse door? Why does her red-hooded raincoat hanging from the metal hook make him believe it was all a dream—that she brought the boat in that night and was developing her film in the makeshift darkroom he had set up for her? Wasn't he supposed to provide a beacon of light and safety? A safe harbor in letter and spirit for ships at sea? To reliably guide those seeking rest on land? Where was Palaemon? Why did he not protect her? Unda wonders: Will the gulls in her photographs flock together and fly in a V formation to the hidden chamber where the sea is keeping her? He wonders: Why does the moonlight leave its cold layers of silver on the oars when he rows out to that spot? Why is there only the icy silence of the indifferent lunar beams washing over the long wooden spears he uses to churn the unchanging water? Why is there no answer from the ancient moon when he begs for the return of his daughter? Did Palaemon decide to frolic that night? Was his dolphin full of mischief? Did it lead him astray and seal his daughter's fate?

Each night Unda asks the endlessness of dream time to let him reach back to save his daughter. Each night he pleads with the myriad points of distant star light to erase all the dimensions of today and yesterday. As if through a magician's old wooden box could Unda be sent into the hidden and unknowable landscape of his dreaming daughter's mind. He wants transport back to that solemn night so long ago. He desires to slip into Lumen's dream the way a cool, autumn ocean breeze nudges its way through the cracks in the lighthouse stone. The way tiny bubble crabs slip silently under the sand. Unda asks the impassive ocean to show him how he can enter his frightened daughter's dream about the ill-fated seagull. "Here!" he wants to tell her. "Look, here!" In his arms. He wants to show her. The bird is safe now. "See!" he tells her. "Here's the gull in my arms! Here!" Her dream is far away. So far away.

He cannot reach it.

CAPE COD TIMES

LITTLE BREWSTER ISLAND

Mishap or Suicide?

LITTLE BREWSTER ISLAND—The investigation into the disappearance at sea last month of Georgia Unda is officially winding down. "Only one of two things could have happened to that girl," said Sheriff Mortifico when questioned by the media yesterday afternoon. "Either she had some sort of accident and fell overboard, or she jumped in, wanting to kill herself, to drown."

Since Ms. Unda's disappearance, there has been some speculation about her mental state and the possibility that she might have been suicidal. Her father, Ralph Unda, had no comment. One of our reporters was chased away from the Boston Light by a handful of fishermen who usually congregate at the local tackle shop. One man, however, offered to speak on condition of anonymity.

"Ain't you media folks got nothing better to do than keep coming back here to hound this grief-stricken man? You people just leave Ralph Unda alone, hear?! Ain't he suffered enough without all you blood sucking people from the newspapers and TV and everybody else getting into this terrible business 'bout it all being 'cause that poor girl mighta been out of her head?! What difference does it make?! She ain't coming back whether she was crazy or no so's how's all this cursed hounding gonna help that poor man? Don't you know enough to just let him be? Just leave that godforsaken man alone. Got enough ghosts swimming around his head. Don't need you journalist fellas poking into his private business. No sir. That's all I got to say, and I'll sign that release paper and you can quote me but I ain't giving you my name. Now git goin'!"

As far as we know, there have been no charges made against Ralph Unda regarding the disappearance of his daughter. Sheriff Mortifico and the Coast Guard have interviewed Unda

on at least three occasions since the night Georgia Unda failed to return to shore. Teams of scuba divers have concluded their search in and around the area where Georgia's boat, the Theseus, was found.

Rumors spread rapidly in small, intimate shore communities like Little Brewster Island. There has been speculation about Georgia Unda's mental health for some time. Yet, out of personal loyalty to Mr. Unda or deep-rooted admiration for his many years of stewardship as the lighthouse keeper of the Boston Light, no one will confirm or deny whether or not mental illness played a role in the denouement of this tragedy.

Cape Cod mothers
Don't bake no pies,
Heave away, haul away!
They feed their children
Codfish eyes.
And we're bound away for Australia!

"Funny you should sing that part right now!"
"About mothers and no pies ya mean?"
"She up and left him y'know."
"You mean Mrs. Unda?!"
"Early this morning. Before light."
"You don't say!"
"A long time comin' it was."
"For sure."
"Too much to bear I suppose. A dead child."
"And a husband off the beam."
"For sure."
"Too much to bear."
"It was a long time comin'."
"Wonder if this gonna push poor Ralph over the side."
"You mean like his daughter? Like Lumen?"
"Could be. Could be enough to do it."
"To do himself in? Like Lumen?"
"Too much to bear."

Waving in the decomposition of death like a sea anemone hiding its vicious poison the arms of hope and time unite in my enveloping waves my seas and oceans stitch the dreams of man the way huge nets ensnare struggling crab claws clacking to no avail muffled by dark wet death silenced the way Lumen's precious seagull was silenced so I torment Unda each wave I send to crash against the rocks turns into a thousand demon splashes scurrying up the lighthouse entering Unda's bedroom and filling his night's dreamscape with the endless repeating horror of Lumen lost forever Lumen holding the seagull's lifeless body swaying deep in my waters wings uselessly out as if in flight as if the back and forth sway were the slow motion movement of a ballerina's arms bending and stretching and Lumen stares at her father her flesh glowing as if coated with a white phosphorus gel but nothing in the eyes except an intolerable stare like a mannequin under a light bulb or a face on a billboard illuminated by the headlights of a speeding truck Lumen stares at her father with the fixity and indifference of ancient rock with the tormented helplessness of a frightened child everything that mankind agonizes over floats through the windows of his dwellings and sinks my vastness swallowing every moment every grief every aspiration nothing will reanimate the mechanical stumbling of Lumen's corpse like a puppet weightlessly dangling at the ends of its strings do you see Unda? do you wish in your sleep of knives that you could slice out your eyes to finally see no more do you see Unda? see how the circles and semicircles of mourning fish like rainbows of garlands wrap themselves around Lumen's listing body see their sorrow? see your lost daughter on the black seafloor the bottom of my cavernous heart see her clutching her obsession the seagull that beckoned to her feverish mind see her Unda see how she dove off the boat to rescue this flailing phantom do you hear the desperate thrashing of Lumen's struggling limbs enveloped by my invisible arms of liquid fury you try to comfort her but the blanket you gently settle upon her child's bed becomes my cold pummeling suffocating waves and you tell her over and over she is not responsible her dream did not doom the found seagull but I have created a whirlpool of confusion sorrow and death nothing in the feeble reasoning of mankind can challenge my remorseless eternal energy so look at this Unda you must look and hear I have made an endless floating graveyard of Lumens bobbing like hundreds of buoys to and fro back and forth and she is a different age each one is your daughter holding the seagull twisted in death see her Unda in every age of her short life and in the ages that would have come see her Unda in the last visage floating above at the horizon an old thing covered in white strands of rotting seaweed her gray and white hair matted like wet clay across the breast of the gull and the moon mocks you Unda it bathes her in its sterile silver glow the moon mocks you it will not let you look away.

> The sea gave up the dead that were in it,
> and death and Hades gave up the dead that
> were in them, and each person was judged
> according to what they had done.
>
> Then I saw "a new heaven and a new
> Earth," for the first heaven and the first earth
> had passed away, and there was no longer any
> sea.
>
> There is the sea, vast and spacious,
> teeming with creatures beyond number—living
> things both large and small.

...that's how it remained...after that night...my sweet Lumen lost to me...I tried so hard to comfort you...I could not bring your mind back to the innocent sleep of that night...before your dream...after you found that dead bird there was an empty dark corner in your soul... your irrational thoughts created the savage waves that would devour you years later...you were in a nameless place of endless sorrow...I tried...sweet

Lumen...the way that little boy at the water fountain tried so compassionately to relieve some of my grief on the night of my grandfather's wake... the dead seagull awakened some kind of ancient obsessive power in you... an emotional plague waiting to be activated...a pandemic of irrational guilt and grief...buried somewhere in the most primitive...powerful layer of your psyche...I had hoped that as you grew a little older and developed a keen interest in photography,...that the creative dimensions of image-making might neutralize or somehow diffuse the worst elements of what you conjured to torment yourself...even the doctors agreed that some therapeutic value might be derived from your involvement with photography...but somehow your photographs became a vehicle for your obsessions...they enlarged and expanded them...as if the toxicity in your imagination found a complicit partner in the lens of your camera...at first I thought you were getting it out of your system...the countless photographs of the lighthouse...of the rocks...of the seagulls...especially all the seagulls...but it gradually turned into a kind of nightmarish hall of mirrors...lining the lighthouse walls with photographs of the seagulls...at dawn...at dusk...especially at dusk...that's when you put out on the Theseus...that night...just as dusk began to slowly melt into dissolving pink and orange blankets...oh...my Lumen...my sweet...caring little girl...you did not bring harm to that unfortunate bird because of your innocent child's dream...it was the work of nature...it was the wind's work...for days I took you by the hand and walked around the lighthouse...across the rocks...down to the sea at low tide and back...so you could feel the wind...how it whips around...especially in March...when you had the dream and discovered the gull...as it grew a little warmer...I left your windows partially open...so you could hear the wind wrapping itself around the lighthouse...see...my dearest one...it's just the wind...do you hear it?...do you hear it?...does the wind blow through the delicate mist of your spirit?...does the wind blow your invisible hair into your eyes?...do you hear it?...do you hear it?...

Constantly asking what he is unable to answer. Unda trying to escape his thoughts of that night. The horror and sorrow of what he cannot change assembling and reassembling in his mind, like a jigsaw puzzle exploding into thousands of pieces that fall back into place in slow motion before bursting apart over and over. Each piece becomes another of the questions Unda cannot answer. Another particle of guilt and remorse; another dimension of his endless grief. The torture of a parent who could not save his child.

Why didn't Lumen's doctors see how dangerous her obsessions were? That her thoughts about the dead seagull could one day make her suicidal? Why couldn't they see her interest in photography would only justify and deepen her irrational guilt? Why can't Unda forgive himself for encouraging her? For buying her the camera equipment? Each night he asks the wind: Why were your hands so powerful that night? Staring at the sea, standing on the lighthouse terrace, the sting of the salt air blending with his tears, he asks the wind: Why couldn't you slip into my child's dream and tell her that sometimes a bird may suffer from your forceful blows? Why, begs Unda, didn't you leave us alone that night? Why didn't you blow and rattle far above Boston Lights? Why did you seal my poor daughter's fate that night? Why did you send a gull to its death? Why did Lumen have to find it, and make it her private, hellish tragedy? Why did the sirens not appear by the lighthouse, to lure the wind into impenetrable rock? To break the body of the sinister wind into scattering, confused tiny molecules? Where were the sirens' deceitful melodies that night? Where was their song that might have hypnotized the winds? To make them crash and splinter upon the rocks like the countless ships of centuries past? Why didn't schools of fish entwine themselves around Lumen, after she jumped off the Theseus? Why didn't the fish form a floating blanket with their rainbow skin, to ferry Lumen back to shore and the safety of the dry lighthouse? Why didn't a calm and noble leviathan rise to the surface with stately elegance, causing huge waves to carry Lumen back to land? Why couldn't the gull have been merely stunned, so its wings would flap and brush away Lumen's tears? Why didn't the morning wind beg Lumen for forgiveness? Why didn't the crabs lock claws together to form a necromantic union and conjure an ancient spell from the sea to bring the gull back to life? Looking in the mirror with despair every morning, Unda asks his reflection "Why am I still here? Why can't I die in my sleep and find Lumen? Why can't I find her? Why can't I find my Lumen?"

For me, my father, you have the reach and power of Oceanus, forever protecting all.

Each night I float through your dreams with soothing hands.

In your troubled slumber, in the rubbery darkness of your mind.

Like frenzied deck hands tossing cargo overboard.

To prevent the ship from sinking.

I try each night to erase your self-condemnation.

The endless sorrow of your restless mind.

I shape the magical clay of wet sand into thousands of seagulls.

Send them in circles that spin around the lighthouse.

Do you see, Father?

See the happy energy of their evolving flight?

They engulf the lighthouse like endless rings of white leaves.

Each bird nods respectfully as they pass your window.

As though they are priests bowing to the cross during Mass.

Their brilliant white feathers dappled with stained glass rainbows.

The colors of the glass windows in the church walls.

All for you, all for you.

I send them all for you to erase your torment.

To show you that my death was like a squall.

The same inevitability.

That same irreversible act as in the worst of nature's forces.

The worst of what a floundering mind will believe.

Please do not devour yourself like Ouroboros.

"Them Coast Guard fellas still at it?"

"For sure. Could be two, maybe more boats."

"I was watchin' from my porch this morning."

"You'd think that poor girl's body would be found already."

"Been hours now."

"For sure. No sign of her."

"Seems that way."

"Something wrong with that girl."

"Ever since she found that dead gull on the rocks."

"Something took a hold of her."

"Like she was possessed."

"Possessed! Right! That's the word I been lookin' for."

"Like something took her over!"

"That's for sure."

"And nothing in the world could change it."

"Felt so sorry for poor Unda."

"Being the parent of a disturbed child."

"Me too. Felt damn sorry for the man."

"But the girl was fine, that's the hell of it."

"That's right. She was as happy as the sunrise."

"It was almost like a curse."

"Finding that dead seagull?"

"Yeah, and the dream."

"And nothing in the world could change it."

"Nothing in the world."

"Unda started takin' her to them shrink doctors."

"Tryin' to figure out why she got so obsessed."

"That gull flew into the lighthouse."

"Poor fellow. Unda must have told us a hundred times."

"Somehow Lumen thought it was her fault."

"Never made no sense at all."

"No sense."

"Like there was a tragedy waiting in her."

"Waiting to come out."

"That's for sure."

"This here talk is gettin' too depressing!"

"Let's hear a little of that shanty!"

"It'll lift our spirits!"

"'So heave her up, me bully bully boys!'"

"There you go!"

"Heave away, haul away!"

"And what's next?"

"'Heave her up, why don't you make some noise?'"

"Why don't you make some noise? And we're—"

"Bound away for Australia!"

"There you go!"

"We're bound away for Australia!"

The moon mocks you Unda bathing her in its sterile silver glow the moon mocks you it controls your gaze you cannot look away all of your movements all of your gestures like the twirling strands of seaweed tumbling and twisting within the foam of endless waves because I am endless eternal as your regret has no limit unbounded like my mysteries and my secrets the rotting particles of lost ships like wandering souls in a hopeless dance on the blackness of my lowest depths no Unda your precious Lumen belongs to me your vigil at the peak of your useless lighthouse is the pathetic ritual of a forgotten man as if a pebble were trying to become a mountain you are forever inefficient always incomplete I change the shore with my giant liquid fingers always rising and falling upon the sand always seducing ships great and small as I seduced your beautiful Lumen I let her see my hypnotic shifting motion I let her mind become my illusions and her eyes obeyed what they commanded you sorrowful lighthouse keeper all keepers throughout the lighthouses of the world do you think I can be deterred do you think your watchfulness robs my powers my sovereignty some lives some ships may be guided to safety when I choose to be calm there are times when I sleep when I am still but do not forget the thieves do not rejoice one thief was damned just as your sweet Lumen was sentenced to death by her own innocence the conjured image of the dying seagull led your daughter to her death as she jumped over the side to save the bird existing only in her tortured mind she heard the frenzied flapping and flailing of the drowning bird's wings and she leapt and the wings slapping against me slapping helplessly against my wet green face all this was the affirmation of my will the end of Lumen's feverish dreams of guilt and the beginning of your hellish despair all clocks in the world have surrounded you in countless concentric circles like the rings of my sea embrace as Lumen struggled no more her lungs full of me descended like a dream like the slow motion of a dream and the clocks like the perfect rings of ever widening enclosure and the clocks smirk at you Unda they have no sympathy they are bound by nature torrential downpours that shake the ground with relentless hammering then cease into silence before the pounding and roar of thunder resume yes the clocks show midnight because that is when Lumen jumped she leapt over the side do you see how the spirits of the gulls glide over her bed their shadows intersecting and dividing into the squares of fishing nets waving flapping geometry of the entangled shadows trying in vain to go back to that night of troubled sleep trying to find a way into Lumen's dream hoping to change what became an endless horrific sorrow see how their shadows crisscross and zigzag in terrible despair and pitiful fury trying to find Lumen's dream to give her solace to see them flying to see them alive to rescue her mind from despair and desperation she is with me Unda she is eternally bound to me at the bottom on the seafloor I invite her as though it were my home she is in my possession for all time my seafloor has become her stage did you know Unda her only solace is to perform that terrible night scene and the storm and your useless lighthouse and in these repeating scenarios she carries a lantern she looks up at you standing on the top of the lighthouse gesticulating in a frenzied pantomime of frustration she lowers her head Unda do you see her sorrow she knows you cannot help the lighthouse means nothing it saves nothing she is ashamed of you Unda do you see do you recognize her blanched corpse flopping about like a collapsed puppet flipped and nudged by gusts of wind her lantern glow becomes her face she moves through the storm carrying her own incandescent face in the rectangle dripping with the rain mixed with tears as if they were a blood offering of her body returning to me with innocence and resignation succumbing to my unchanging and unalterable being all of your efforts all of your vows all of your desires collected and suffocated surrounded and confused you are the unfortunate mouse that scurries along the top of a grain silo and falls deep into the mass below imbedded surrounded by it and none of the frantic squeals of the mouse are heard as the grain like my waves giddily slapping at midnight envelop and pull this doomed creature dying foolish and careless and forgotten.

Unda hoped that as Lumen began her teenage years, the obsessions and nightmares would fade away. But she did not recover. Her mental and emotional stability was constantly besieged by the dark, irrational belief that she alone had caused the seagull's death. Unda began having nightmares of the Gerome painting *The Christian Martyr's Last Prayer*. In these demented visions, he saw his daughter in the circle of crucified victims. Each hapless figure was Lumen, the agony on her face amplified from cross to cross. Men and women huddled together, uttering their last prayer before the lions were let loose, the humans transformed in Unda's desperate dream into gulls. As the birds feverishly recited their final utterances, the lions slowly dissolved into his lighthouse. The lighthouse, bearing lions' fang and claws, would rip the doomed gulls, tear their bodies to shreds of white splashed with their blood, like the countless drawings Unda often found in Lumen's room, drawings of gulls sliced into tiny pieces of white drawing paper, streaked with Lumen's blood shed as she ferociously wielded the scissors, sticky with her blood, the flurry of red paper bits like demonic snow.

As the doctors and psychiatrists offered less and less hope for the return of Lumen's rational faculties, her ghastly visions became more and more of a nightly visitation for Unda. On some nights he awoke suddenly, his bedclothes drenched in sweat. He'd rush into the bathroom and try to wash off the lion's paw mud, mixed with the blood and sand from the arena, to wipe away Lumen's blood. On some nights, it was the painting itself that haunted him. Instead of entering the scene depicted in the ghastly painting, Unda's malignant dream visions had him racing down endless spirals of lighthouse steps, leaping three and four at a time, one frantic jump after another, knowing he must leave the lighthouse onto the surrounding rocks to prevent Lumen from discovering the seagull. In the hot hysteria of these variations on the original dreams in the arena, Unda saw it hanging on every wall at every landing, paintings and landings impossibly duplicated and repeating infinitely, as he jumped and ran down the lighthouse steps, with the insane accumulation of the paintings following him, pursuing him, reappearing endlessly, always there again and again as Unda turned to descend the next flight of stairs, never reaching the bottom, never being able to rush out of the lighthouse and protect his daughter.

**CAPE CODE TIMES
LITTLE BREWSTER ISLAND**

A Parent's Despair

LITTLE BREWSTER ISLAND—Recent inquiries have revealed that Georgia Unda, the young woman who disappeared at sea last year, had exhibited signs of mental illness for most of her life. Unnamed sources have shed light on what appears to have been an irrational obsession that haunted the unfortunate girl since childhood. Her father, Ralph Unda, became visibly agitated and almost violent when approached by one of our reporters with questions about his daughter's mental health. While most of the residents in the surrounding area refused to volunteer any information about the girl, several individuals who had known "Lumen" (as she was called by her father) stepped forward. They confirmed she suffered from delusions that began around the age of eight. Apparently, the girl believed that a dream she had one night caused the death of a seagull she found the following morning. In her dream, a seagull was buffeted by strong storm winds, causing it to slam against the lighthouse and fall to its death. The girl remained unshakably convinced that her dream had caused the death of the gull.

Our anonymous source also confirmed that for fifteen years, Unda brought his daughter to doctors and psychiatrists hoping that some kind of therapy and medication would rid her of this morbid, self-destructive belief. The same source, who has lived in the area for many years and knew Unda quite well, emphasized the toll this had taken on Unda himself. The distraught father aged considerably during this time. Some townspeople and neighbors saw him going to and from the lighthouse frequently. An unidentified man from the tackle shop told us that Unda sank into an oblivion of sorrow after Lumen disappeared at sea. The man clung to the hope that his daughter would recover even though one could clearly see how the emotional stress of watching his precious Lumen fade farther away from reality made the poor man look like a ghost of

himself. According to this same individual, after Lumen's disappearance and presumed death, Unda's behavior lost all semblance of normalcy. He took the boat out every night to the same spot, Lumen had left it. These actions certainly stemmed from a parent's despair.

"Can't figure it no how!"

"I know what ya mean."

"How a man could refuse to come to his daughter's funeral Mass. Don't make any sense."

"Maybe that was the last straw for his wife."

"Could be so! Could be so!"

"I mean, I know it was because Lumen was declared dead, like in an official way I mean, 'cause they never found her body."

"I know what you mean. It was the mother's way of letting go and saying goodbye."

"Having that Mass."

"Puttin' an end to the misery."

"For sure, for sure."

"And as I recollect, she left Unda not too long after. Ain't that so?"

"It was around that time, after the Mass and all."

"My wife knew Mrs. Unda socially. You know, they was on friendly terms and had little get-togethers now and again for coffee or shopping."

"I seen them at times around here in town."

"Well, she told my missus how hard it was to deal with Lumen's death and how Ralph, you know, Unda, was so far gone with grief he wasn't the same man no more."

"Not one bit, that's for sure."

"He almost never spoke to her and seemed to be fading away a little more every day. She said he couldn't accept Lumen being gone."

"Felt like it was his fault somehow, 'cause it happened at sea."

"For sure! Being the lighthouse keeper, it was a tragedy he should have prevented."

"What a torment to himself that must be."

"You betcha. Poor man. It totally consumed him. Sucked all the reason and soul right out of him."

"For sure, for sure."

"What a torment."

"Poor man."

"Sucked the soul right out of him."

"You betcha."

"For sure."

...my daughter...my sweet precious girl...no one can see as I can see... I must find a way to rescue you...to bring you back from this toxic obsession...it's eating away at you dear Lumen...can't you see that?...you did nothing...you were asleep...safely asleep while your imagination controlled your thoughts...it was a storm...you must have been thinking of the storm...how the wind was bending and whipping...how the rain pummeled the observatory glass like thousands of pebbles...was it because I scolded you at the circus?...did you think the lighthouse was being attacked?...that the lions' sharp slaws were hammering at the glass?...it was only the storm my helpless delicate daughter...my holy incantation...sweet proof of a loving God...how can I reach you?...to find some surcease in the darkened rooms where you withdraw more and more...nothing seems or speaks in an honest way...these are all tortured lies my Lumen...lies which beckon to you...please Oh please do not believe them...your dream that night was itself but a shadow...how I've wished and begged the lighthouse could enter your sleep...to sail through your shadows and disfigured notions of guilt...I would steer the lighthouse as if it were a Trireme...to rescue you...to unlock the sealed chamber of your self-created guilt...and all the doctor's ask the same questions but none could probe into that hidden chamber where you kept your morbid secrets...Oh my Lumen...how I wish I could break down the door of that chamber...to reach in...reach in with strong arms and clear eyes...whisk you away into the calm morning light...the light after...and all would be serene and still...the fury of winds and rain...all gone...only the bending blankets of innocent morning light...was there some kind of dormant malignancy imbedded in your soul?...it was as if your whole being was taken over that day you found the seagull...so frightening to see you that way and be unable to undo what your mind built...the doctors didn't know...I remember the first time one of them talked about schizophrenia...that it had remained hidden...waiting for some kind of trigger to emerge and slowly take over your personality...the way you saw the world...the way your sense of reason was gradually contaminated by chaos and fantasies...I remember that first doctor's words... two months after you discovered the dead gull and it became painfully clear that your thoughts and feelings were abnormally deep...abnormally intense...I can still hear the doctor's words...Mr. Unda, we feel Lumen's obsessions about the deceased seagull are the symptoms, the outward manifestation of her condition. This could have happened earlier, when she was six or seven, and it could have remained submerged within her psyche until her twenties or thirties. Schizophrenia is very cruel in this regard: it destroys the brain's ability to be objective and rational. But for the person afflicted, their way of seeing the world is the only reality they know. They never see that what they believe is a delusion. What they believe is a delusion. A delusion. Delusion...delusion...that last night...the night you took the Theseus out and leapt into the black water...I saw your face in the moonlight...your eyes were calm...you had decided to do what you had wanted to do for so long...but I should have known...I should have looked deeper into the calm message of your eyes...like the scan of the lighthouse beam reaching across the sea...my Lumen...why didn't I understand...why couldn't I see in that moment the serenity in your gaze was made out of a final resolve to end your life?...

If only I could have summoned Keto to frighten away the storm and keep the seagull safe.

The chaos of my thoughts became a daily torment for you.

My eyes only saw the lies my mind conceived.

If only we could make time refund the sorrow we spend.

Each night I beg the wind to sculpt sweet sea soft kisses for you.

Can you see me in your dreams?

I ride Archelon with glowing gold coins for eyes.

The secret treasures of a thousand sunken ships offer themselves to me.

I know how badly you wanted to rescue me from madness.

But no malignant creatures swim in my waters.

No fearful shadows swarming across the ocean floor.

My mind is no longer swollen by the fevers of unreason.

I had to die so that my innocence could be reawakened.

O my sweet father please understand I am at peace now.

Somehow my discordant dream and the dead seagull formed a bridge
inside my soul.

Do not lay blame or responsibility upon your head.

No sanity or logic was mixed into the mortar that made this bridge.

It might have been a mysterious lineage of spiritual sorrow.

It might have been the hidden destiny of my being and my mind.

Do not blame yourself for these things you could not control.

Do not let my final act also drown your memories of my untroubled
childhood.

Oh dearest father do not turn the lighthouse into your executioner.

Do not be the trapdoor of the gallows you have built for yourself.

"Still can't figure why he lost all common sense over it, like
something took all the reason out of his head."

"Like he couldn't accept it, I mean, Lumen's suicide and all?"

"He stopped seeing things for what they was 'stead of getting

all carried away with his delusions—I guess that's what they call it."

"For sure."

"Anyways, it ain't just about the girl dying and Unda blaming hisself, I mean, I seen he was warped and wrapped up in this kind of thinking when that whole thing started—"

"The dead bird, you mean?"

"Right, when that whole thing started. It was plain as day, sorry to say, there was something definitely wrong with that child."

"Plain as day."

"Gotta be a parent to know how desperate Unda musta felt. Them head doctor visits never gave him any hope, none that anybody could see."

"My boy was in Lumen's elementary class. Used to get the chills

just sittin' near that girl."

"My sister's twins were in arts class with Lumen in high school."

"That was it! For sure. Every damn drawing or painting that poor lost soul made was another picture of herself at the lighthouse, holding that damned dead seagull and crying."

"Now, when she went off to college, wasn't Unda always talkin' 'bout how she started getting interested in photography..."

"That's right!"

"He thought it was a good sign."

"For sure."

"And even them docs chimed in that

taking pictures was a kind of therapy."

"For Lumen you mean?"

"Yeah."

"But she kept right on with all the craziness anyway."
"Photography did no good for her."

"Not if you consider the downright tragic fact that all the pictures she ever

took were of seagulls!"

"That's true for sure!"

"Like the photographs made her worse."

"Added another level

to her crazy obsession."

"Poor Unda. How he cherished that girl."

"The hopelessness of it."

"Poor man."

"Sucked the soul right out of him."

> Thy was in the sea, And they paths in
> the mighty waters, And they footprints may
> not be known.

> It was you who split open the sea by
> your power; you broke the heads of the monster
> in the waters.

As Lumen became more obsessed with irrational beliefs, Unda's grasp of everyday reality became more tenuous. He began having nightmares, all of which reflected, in one way or another, his refusal to accept the psychiatrists' unanimous diagnosis that his daughter was hopelessly and irretrievably schizophrenic. In one of the most disturbing nightmares, the doctors were bare-chested rowers in the bowels of a Clipper ship. They chanted in unison as they rowed: Unda could not save her! Unda could not save her! The dream concluded the same way each night, with Unda almost slipping off his sweat-drenched pillow, Unda at the wheel of the Theseus, trying in vain to steer clear of the menacing Clipper ship. Every therapy session Lumen had, from the time her attachment to the dead gull began at the age of eight, was depicted across the skies, in monstrously enlarged, distorted proportions. In each of the phantasmagorical murals, the psychiatrist or therapist interviewing her became large and larger, as Lumen became smaller and smaller. The gigantic scenes stretched across the horizon as though a cursed colossus of Rhodes had abandoned his protective duties, letting the Rhodians fall to Demetrius. So there was no valor in Unda's dream, no ascension to the nobility and peace of higher acts. Some of these monumental panels reverberated with flashes of lightning accompanied by cavernous peals of thunder and pounding rain, mocking Unda's inability to save his daughter by mimicking the effects of the harsh weather that surrounded Lumen and the boat that night. "Lumen's fate was being symbolically acted out by your nightmares, Mr. Unda. I know the loss of your daughter has tragic proportions for you and your wife, but you must try and realize that Lumen's psychosis was like a kind of psychic cancer. It continued feeding on itself for years. Flashes of lucidity would always be followed by morbid relapses into schizophrenic delusions about the seagull. Changing from one psychiatrist to another would offer some variation of the diagnosis or differences in medication and therapy. It seemed to Unda, especially during Lumen's childhood when the obsession began, that each doctor would ultimately declare the girl was incurable, after first suggesting their way of "treating her was a mistaken evaluation of the disorder, Mr. Unda. The specialists on our staff believe that your daughter's dream about the dead seagull produced a kind of waking somnambulance, a form of self-hypnosis that, we believe, can be penetrated and cured by electro-convulsive shock therapy. The first thing we must do" is to find a way for Unda to regain some normalcy in his life, but it was not to be. The nightmares raged and roared through his helpless mind. He was lost in an abyss of unconsciousness and terror as if the enormous tentacles of the Kraken described by Pontoppidan pulled him to the bottom of the sea. Unda's nightmares were always changing and transmogrifying in hideous ways. The worst of this self-accusatory image-making, was a singularly horrifying nightmare in which Unda himself had become the lighthouse. Like an embalmed corpse or a sleepwalking zombie, he took leaden steps through the sea, a Fachan whose one eye was the lighthouse beam and with only one leg, Fachan became literally half of a human being, just as

Unda no longer saw himself as a complete person. He could not save his daughter, could not return her to the untroubled innocence of childhood. The greatest sorrow of Unda's life was that he could not rescue his daughter's mind, could not stitch those ever-dwindling moments of Lumen's rational mind into a fabric of sanity and peace. As the months seamlessly dissolved into years, like a paralyzed man watching his house burn down, Unda saw how madness reached into Lumen's soul with obscenely probing fingers, destroying her reason and forever crippling the happiness of her young life. Some nights, Unda's nightmarish journeys delivered him to a kind of dark tribunal in which rows of hooded judges sat at a fantastically long table. The mournful, elongated cry of multiple fog horns could be heard, first low as if from a distant shore. Gradually, the volume increased and became so loud that the vibrations shook the table as well as the somber figures seated there. One by one, the hoods were swept back by a sudden gust of wind, a wild gale from a dangerous storm. Each hood flew back to reveal not a human being but the battered and bloody head of a seagull. Each bird fixed Unda in its angry stare, full of resentment and hatred, as if even in death the gulls sat in judgement, implacable in their black solemn robes, forever judging him, forever blaming him for Lumen's fixation, always reminding him of his failure to perform his duty as the lighthouse keeper, his inability to rescue her sanity, to soothe her dreams from that cursed night with comfort and reassurance, with paternal embracing light.

> For thou hast cast me into the deep,
> in the midst of the seas; and the
> floods compassed me about; all the
> billows and thy waves passed over me.
>
> In his hand are the depths of the
> earth, and the mountain peaks belong
> to him. The sea is His, for He made
> it, and his hands formed the dry land.

CAPE COD TIMES
LITTLE BREWSTER ISLAND

Reunited In Death

LITTLE BREWSTER ISLAND—The Coast Guard issued a statement today declaring that Ralph Unda is lost at sea. No body was recovered after divers inspected the area where the Theseus was found drifting two nights ago. Our readers may recall that Mr. Unda was the lighthouse keeper on Little Brewster Island and that his daughter, Georgia, an apparent suicide victim, disappeared in the same manner several years ago. No official conclusion was ever made regarding Lumen, as she was affectionately called by her father. At the time she went missing, also aboard the Theseus, she was in her early twenties.

Anonymous sources disclosed how the burden of dealing with Lumen's mental state took its toll on the Undas' marriage and ultimately, on Mr. Unda. He refused to attend the funeral mass for Lumen arranged by his wife one year after the daughter's disappearance at sea. Mrs. Unda moved not long afterwards. One of the townspeople who did not want to be identified told us that Lumen's wife could no longer tolerate her husband's fantasy life. He was incapable of rationally processing his daughter's death and would not give up the mentally disturbed belief that he should have rescued her. We touched upon this in our previous piece in which we stated that Unda's sanity had gradually deteriorated to the point where he held the purely fantastical belief that he must somehow rescue Lumen. Sources from the Coast Guard informed us that Unda's behavior became more and more irrational, noting that after his daughter's funeral mass, he began a nightly routine of taking the Theseus to the same spot where Lumen had left it on the night she disappeared. It was observed that after returning from these nocturnal outings, Unda could be seen at the top of the lighthouse, standing at the railing with the giant beam of light from the Fresnel lens just above his head, fixed in the same position until dawn, scanning the sea with binoculars. By this

point, Unda must have suffered a total breakdown. He no longer spoke to anyone in the town and seemed to be in a somnambulistic state, seemingly unaware of his surroundings, and existing only for the purpose of taking out the Theseus each night and inspecting the dark sea from the top of the lighthouse.

A longtime resident of the town gave permission for the following quote on condition of anonymity. Although nothing can reverse all the tragedies that have plagued the Unda family, these compassionate words from a close friend may offer some comfort:

"If ya ask me, I'd say it's best if you news fellas just let my friend Unda alone. He's at peace where he's at. Just leave him be. He's with his daughter. With Lumen. I been his friend for lots of years.

Ain't never been no father who loved his daughter like he done. He lived for that child. Worshipped her. It was like another part of his soul came alive whenever he was with her. Poor man spent a fortune takin' that girl to doctors after she got all obsessed about that seagull dyin.' He just wouldn't accept it, her mind goin' I mean. He went clear out of his head when she grew up and killed herself that night, jumpin' off the boat. I knew he wouldn't find peace till he joined her, till he dove off the boat, to find her, be with his light, his Lumen. Just let my friend alone. Leave him alone. He's with Lumen."

So I finally envelop you Unda we are united in eternal embrace you no longer belong to the land and the air your lungs filled with my ancient water here there is no need for breath now you must release your mind from the great resentment and anger you have felt about me you have hated me because your precious Lumen chose to hide from her madness yes because you could not save her and because she wanted to be released from the warm daylight from the sustaining rays of the sun she wanted surcease she wanted to end her thoughts the air itself was mocking you the need to breathe had become a form of self-negation so you are one with me Unda you have duplicated Lumen's suicidal plunge into my endless cold mysteries my darkness has no need of the comforts of land there is no light in my depths nothing that resonates with the logic or the comforts of the world above the surface do you see the dozens of sea horse skeletons do you see them now how they perform a macabre dance for you lined in a row turning their heads left and right like a deranged Can-Can all of it to ridicule your futility and uselessness an imitation of the way you nervously shifted your lantern back and forth left and right shining the flashing light across the black water at night hoping in your own madness to see a trace of Lumen all these days and weeks and months after she disappeared I can offer you only such disdain I am the sea who commands the shores it is I who allows land and its human inhabitants to go about their lives to prosper and live peacefully until those grave moments when I am angered and send my smashing waves to destroy whatever is within my dangerous reach all of the lighthouses in all the world mean nothing to me they are like blind surgeons leaning over a dying patient hoping to guide their scalpels to the waiting wound do you not see Unda your entire life has become a bitter unanswered supplication you are the blind surgeon you are the blinking lighthouses and in their death throes they sink into darkness I am puzzled Unda you have spent your life watching the sea day and night your lighthouse your surrogate self an alternate version of your life as a man all these years how did you not foresee your helplessness and impotence your sanity evaporating in a desperate struggle against my powers why did you not see there is no reason or justice in me I am eternal energy and mystery the shipwrecks that have sunk into my darkness over thousands of years are too numerous to be counted ships lying on the bottom schools of fish flowing through the holes along their sides like a decaying corpse with eyeless sockets the way fish glide in and out of the poor devil's gaping mouth do you see Unda do you see now everything begins and ends with me my endless caverns of mystery do you hear the repeating chants of all the souls who have perished within my swollen transparent walls can you hear your sweet Lumen's voice she sings in the chant have you heard it Unda swelling and revolving and resonating in your tortured dreams every night since that night when Lumen came home to me this orthodox chant Unda do you recognize it we have seen the true light do you hear your daughter's voice do you see all the drowned souls gathered in ever widening circles like Saturn's rings each face with mouths chanting can you hear them Unda did you think you could escape did you think you could turn my darkness into light do you remember the lights and the jangle of sounds at the circus you scolded Lumen when she dropped her popcorn now my body has absorbed you will millions of gallons of water be enough to wash the gull's blood from Lumen's lovely dress do you see all the sawdust flakes from the trapeze tent floating around your head like confetti Unda only there is no parade no celebratory homecoming you are not a hero basking in the welcoming palm of an adoring crowd but a lifeless white corpse floating without direction or purpose but you are finally home all life begins in my unknowable mysteries from the protocells billions of years ago so you are released from your mission Unda you are not the lighthouse keeper you no longer breathe air I give you the only possible solace your Lumen has found peace at last all chimeras have been dissolved in my endless canyons of primordial darkness take a last look through my overlapping layers a final fleeting dream vision of your lighthouse see how it quivers within my screens of liquid see how it dissolves into a vanishing specter see how its purpose no longer exists.

...I am no longer bound by the laws of the surface world...I am part of your life again my sweet daughter...I brought the Theseus to the same spot...where you leapt that night...it was as if the stars nodded their approval...finally this was the night I could find you and we could be together again...I wonder if you will be wearing your peach and pink dress... so many summer sunsets I stood at the railing at the top of the lighthouse...the glow of the pastel sky...deepened and enriched with the pink of seaside twilight...I waved my hand like a painter pressing his brush against the palette...like a sculptor squeezing out wet shapes from the spinning clay...I wanted to turn the sky into your running form from the day when you wore that dress the first time...in my restless sleep...each night after you jumped off the boat...each time I fitfully tossed the covers away from my sweaty face... pushing the waves away... making the sea obey me...I remember one night I awoke that way...I swept the blankets off the bed ...I smelled salt air...I looked across the bed...still in the grip of the illusion that I was in the ocean...over the spot where you leapt...clawing and pulling at the sheets...my hands slippery with my own perspiration...until wakefulness dissolved the dream and I was only in my bed...I was not there to save you...but I knew we would find each other...I always kept you alive in my heart...you were a lamp for my feet...my dear Lumen...could you see me in my dreams?... many nights I became the seagull...in my desperate helpless dreams I transformed myself and entered your soul like a vile thief...stole your life and your freedom...I glided easily through the black night...like a kite in slow motion...I floated through the open window of your room...you were safely asleep...I hovered above your bed...gently caressed your forehead with my wing...placed a soft kiss on your face...the delicate feathers of my wing caressing you ever so lightly...and in my pitiful dream we were both sustained and elevated by fantasy...you would have no nightmare... no whistling onboard the Theseus when you took her out...we would have had only red skies that night...a beautiful trio of dolphins would have followed the boat...Oh my beloved daughter...my precious Lumen...I know you didn't board the Theseus that night with your left foot first...you must have seen an albatross...did it nod at you gracefully?...did the myriad souls of the sailors it carries bow their heads as well?...I know you would have been cautious and thrown any flowers overboard...you would not have taken the Theseus out on a Friday...your rainbow colored hen tattoos would have glowed under the soft moonlight...remember how we changed the boat's name?...calling her the Theseus...we wrote the boat's old name on a piece of paper and put it in the little wooden box...we burned the box and threw the ashes into the sea...there'd be no spiders on board...venomous devils from bananas...perhaps some of those souls lost at sea took the form of Cormorants...guiding and watching over you...and the Klabautermann would not have let you see him...there would have been no portent of doom...I know Saint Nicholas would be there to calm any storm that might arise...no Flying Dutchman would dare show itself with its unearthly glow...I was Cimon to your Pero...in our Roman Charity you nourished my soul...my Lumen...my light...

How I wish I could have saved you from my darkness when I was an infant.

How I wish I could have born Eve's twenty-three daughters.

I would have joyously bestowed them upon you.

There is no father with greater love for his daughter.

You have given me all and I shall not want for more.

Now that we are in the same world you will see me dance.

Each night the coral plays a splendid elegant waltz.

The seagull glides gracefully around me as he matches the cadence of the music.

We have been practicing the steps in anticipation of your arrival.

There is no more sorrow in me, my sweet endlessly caring father.

There is no more turmoil of the mind nor agony of the soul.

I see the glowing lighthouse reflected in the seagull's eyes.

I see the final peacefulness and serenity in its eyes.

Now you can let your guilt recede like waves at low tide.

Now you can embrace your daughter's true spirit.

No longer are we burdened with dark thoughts and toxic obsessions.

No longer are we tormented by shadows and sounds.

All of rest all of comfort come cradled by the lighthouse glow.

All of innocence all of wonder return me to you as the child I was.

Look at the thousands of gulls filling the night sky like blinking lamps.

Look at their wings confidently flapping in unison with the murmuring fog horns.

Look at my hands finally cleansed of the blood from the one who died that night.

Oh dearest father how can I take away your pain?

High tide almost covers Little Brewster Island, covering the shag rocks, making the Boston Light and the group of little white houses scattered around it look like the smokestacks of a slowly sinking funnel ship. It may be, at least in fanciful minds, the sea taking pity on Unda, at least temporarily, when it reaches up and around, covering the inclined plane of rocks and pebbles, the tangle of seaweed and shells, where Lumen played, the fruity, bright colors of her dress embellished by the sun in a perfectly blue, cloudless sky.

On that bright morning, after Lumen's terrible dream of the seagull, she raced down the lighthouse steps with a furious, mad energy her father had never seen. Almost flying down the spiral staircase, as though she had to outrun the little shadows of her feet. That image of the poor girl never left Unda's mind, Lumen frenziedly trying to separate herself from the shadows, an omen of what was to happen to her mind. He followed her, but it was too late. If he had known that the dead, unfortunate seagull lay just beyond the lighthouse door, he could have scooped it up and somehow prevented her from finding it. But Unda soon discovered the gull's smashed body was like a red sunrise or a Jonah. It portended bad luck, unstoppable bad luck for Lumen.

Shortly before she set sail on that last night, she passed by the bathroom where her father was shaving with the door open. He saw her reflection in the large oval mirror. She smiled briefly as she said the sailor's goodbye:

Fair winds and following seas.

The second part of the saying was scarcely out of his lips as he turned around to say, "Long may your big jib draw." But Lumen had already started down the long helical staircase. When Unda was a boy, he often played in the yard behind his parent's house. One summer afternoon, he saw a yellow caterpillar being eaten alive. Ants were about to cover it completely. In one final, twisting motion, it lifted itself, forming a small spiral. For some reason Unda could not fathom, that image of the caterpillar curling itself in agony made him think of the twisting lighthouse staircase. When he turned back to the mirror there was only the empty wall, bare except for one of Lumen's photographs of seagulls. The fluffy shaving cream was beginning to collapse and flatten on Unda's face. There would be many nights, after Lumen's disappearance, when he would dream of the caterpillar, slowly twirling its dying body, becoming the lighthouse staircase, while rows and rows of little mirrors, all along the bottom of the walls, reflected only emptiness, only empty space, not Lumen's departure as she left on that night, not her quiet smile that flitted so briefly across the bathroom mirror, and throughout all, like foamy blankets of waves in rough seas, his shaving cream undulating and consuming everything.

Soon after Lumen was declared lost at sea, Unda removed all her seagull photographs. At low tide, when large sections of the shag rocks were exposed, he firmly wedged each picture against a layer of rock, securing the black wooden frames with a few stones. Lumen never explained her reason for photographing the seagulls. Unda hoped that the photography would give his daughter some therapeutic benefit, but ultimately it served as an enabler for her obsessions. Nevertheless, he thought the scattered seagull images might form a Fata Morgana, and inverted by this mirage effect, they would appear airborne, flying together above the rocks. He thought Lumen believed her photographs conjured the spirits of the birds. Maybe the illusion of the gulls appearing in the sky would guide her back to shore and maybe she could finally understand. The gull was alive. The gull did not die. So at last all could be well, and her carefree steps could resume. There was nothing left after high tide. All the photographs were covered by the waves, only a few pieces of cracked frame glass.

The wood eventually became dislodged from the photographs which quickly became waterlogged and vanished beneath the sea.

"So Unda's wife gave birth last night?"

"Poor woman. Heard she was in labor for some time."

"She okay?"

"Oh yeah, for sure!"

"For sure!"

"Unda picked her up early this morning."

"Went right back to the lighthouse?"

"Right back."

"A healthy, bright-eyed girl, I hear."

"Sure was!"

"Good for them! Good for them!"

"Never saw Unda so excited! All this year he been like a boy on Christmas Eve!"

"That's right! Good for him!"

"He's gave the girl a nickname, right?"

"'Cause she's his light, he said!"

"Right. Lumen, he's gonna call her!"

"Means light or bright!"

"Latin, right?"

"Oh yeah, for sure!"

"Lumen has a nice sound to it, smooth and peaceful."

"Unda wants to comb her hair with a codfish bone, like in the shanty he's always singin'!"

"You mean this part?"

> They comb their hair
> With a codfish bone.

"That's right! It goes—"

> With a codfish bone,
> And we're bound away for Australia!

"That's the one! For sure! Nothing in the whole world could trouble Unda, singing that shanty and waiting for his precious Lumen to be born!"

> So heave her up, me bully bully boys,
> Heave away, haul away!

"Why don't you make some noise?"

"That's it! C'mon, all of us now!"

Cape Cod girls
Ain't got no combs,
Heave away, haul away!
They comb their hair
With a codfish bone,
And we're bound away for Australia!

"For sure!"
"That's right!"

Dearest One,

Maybe it was meant for me to finally understand the depth and the tragedy of your sorrow. How you were surrounded by the darkness of death and grief. Perhaps your refusal to attend the funeral mass I arranged for our precious Lumen was the result of the numbing pain only you understand. But I must tell you that it is also the final blow. Our bond to one another is irrevocably broken. I wanted the Mass to be more than symbolic. I hoped it would give us some form of closure. But now I realize that not joining me, to say a final goodbye to our daughter, was the unalterable path that your mind and your heart had to take. Although you were not there, your absence spoke to me in many ways. Gradually, you became the very thing that haunted our unfortunate child. How Lumen's unyielding obsessions over the dead bird found a symbiotic counterpart in your emotional self-flagellation, your utterly irrational belief, amplified through the years, that you were somehow responsible for her tragic obsessions, and in some unknowable, mystical way, you had caused the cancerous thoughts that ultimately robbed her sanity. I don't know what caused her mind to lose its connection to reality. It was futile for us to expect some kind of revelation from the doctors. After the first few years, when she was still barely more than a child, I began to accept what had happened to her, to see it as an unalterable thing and to try and give Lumen as much comfort and love as I could. You would tell me that I had given up hope and had abandoned our daughter. This is when our marriage and our love began to be poisoned. You were like a despondent parent who knows his child has an incurable disease, only months to live. Blinded by unconditional love, but wanting miracles even if they came from painful procedures that would cause great discomfort and give the child an extra day or two. This is painful for me to say to you, but it is true that you behaved in the same way, wanting to recapture Lumen's fading personality, no matter how many tests or medical treatments. You refused to accept that Lumen's insanity was destined to occur, whether it was triggered by a dead seagull when she was a little girl, or by something else that broke the seal of her rational mind, letting the full-blown schizophrenia latent since her birth, come flowing out like trapped lava finding an opening in the cracked earth. You saw that lava, erupting and boiling in the steamy ocean. How many nights did you spend like that? All through the night at the top of the lighthouse, looking out upon the waves, looking for traces of Lumen's sanity. What did you see, my tormented, beloved husband? What phantasmagorical, unconquerable sea monsters did you try to slay on those lonely, haunted nights of feverish watchfulness? Did you cower at the feet of Neptune, a tiny human supplicant shuddering with fear, clasping your shaking hands as you begged the king of the sea to return Lumen, to scoop her white, lifeless form from the ocean floor and return her? Or were you Triton? In reversed form, so that your human half remained beneath the sea, and the fish in an upright position, as the anxious and confused navigator, snapping its oily torso to and fro, desperately searching for our daughter? My sweet soulmate, my husband, father of our precious child, in the maelstrom chaos of your mind and your heart, you have become a stranger to me. When you chose not to attend the funeral mass, I felt as though Lumen died a second time. Many nights, I contemplated whether I would leave or stay, wondering if my departure would be justified or serve only as a gravely unfair act against you. I imagined how Lumen must have jumped from the Theseus that night. I saw her pure, tortured heart, beating with unholy excitement as her mind tricked her for the final time, making her believe she saw her poor wounded gull flailing in the black water. Why was she doomed to believe these chimeras? Why was her childhood robbed of its gentle moments, robbed of the joys so freely distributed to children, the way the dawn sun effortlessly sneaks its rays into rooms? It was my heart that flew from my chest and smashed itself against the lighthouse like that doomed seagull? If only I could have substituted my living heart for the dead bird. I wanted to take Lumen back into my womb, to dance with her inside me, dance on the lighthouse terrace, on the sparkling moonlit shore, to somehow summon all those lost at sea, lost in storms and battles since the Khufu ship, to give my unborn child the purity of Tiamat and the ferocity of Poseidon. My *beloved, you were never able to see what I could see. You could not see that our angelic child somehow found a strange and tragic path that led her away from us. I still dream of the gentle orange dance, of the circle of candles around our bed, on the night we conceived the delight of our lives, our precious Lumen. I still hope that in death, at last in final, peaceful rest, she found some way to harmonize her thoughts, to bring happiness into her confused, tormented soul. I still remember when you first took charge of the lighthouse. You were full of pride and strength when I became pregnant with Lumen, and the guardian of the sea, you were the keeper of the lighthouse. I still regret the times we brought Lumen to the doctors for their endless examinations and tests, their contradictory conclusions, their useless ministrations which pushed our daughter deeper and deeper into her closed, ugly world, never to emerge and be herself again. I still pray for you, my love, and I leave you with this last psalm. May it calm your hopeless soul.*

Oh God our Father, I am surrounded by the
darkness of death and grief.

I am unsure of my steps; the path is hidden
and unknown; the journey seems endless.

But you have promised to be a lamp for my feet,
a light for my path.

Give me the strength to keep my lamp burning.
Turn my darkness into light.

Today. Tomorrow. Til the end of the age.

About the Author

Peter J. Dellolio was born in New York City in 1956. He attended Nazareth High School and New York University and graduated in 1978 with a BA in Cinema Studies and a BFA in Film Production. His poetry, prose-poems, fiction, short plays, artwork, and critical essays have been published in over eighty literary magazines, journals, and anthologies. His poetry collections are: *A Box Of Crazy Toys* (2018, Xenos Books/Chelsea Editions), *Bloodstream Is An Illusion Of Rubies Counting Fireplaces* (2023), and *Roller Coasters Made of Dream Space* (2023, Cyberwit/Rochak Publishing). Chapters from his critical study of Alfred Hitchcock (*Hitchcock's Cinematic World: Shocks of Perception and the Collapse of the Rational*) have appeared in *The Midwest Quarterly Literature/Film Quarterly*, *Kinema*, *Flickhead*, and *North Dakota Quarterly*. *Dramatika Press* published a volume of his one-act plays. From this collection, *The Seeker* appeared in an issue of *Collages*

& Bricolages, and *Stopping On One's Way* was recently published in *Synchronized Chaos Journal*. Dellolio is contributing editor for *NYArts Magazine*, where he writes art and film reviews; he also wrote monographs on several new artists. He was Co-Publisher/Editor-in-Chief of *Artscape2000*, a prestigious, award-winning art e-zine. He has taught poetry and art for *LEAP* and continues to work as an artist. His paintings and 3D works offer abstract images of famous people in all walks of life who have died tragically at a young age. Peter J. Dellolio lives in Brooklyn. Find him at *www.saatchiart.com/peterdellolio.com*.

www.ingramcontent.com/pod-product-compliance
Lightning Source LLC
Chambersburg PA
CBHW061552310726
48972CB00008B/2728